The Blue Light

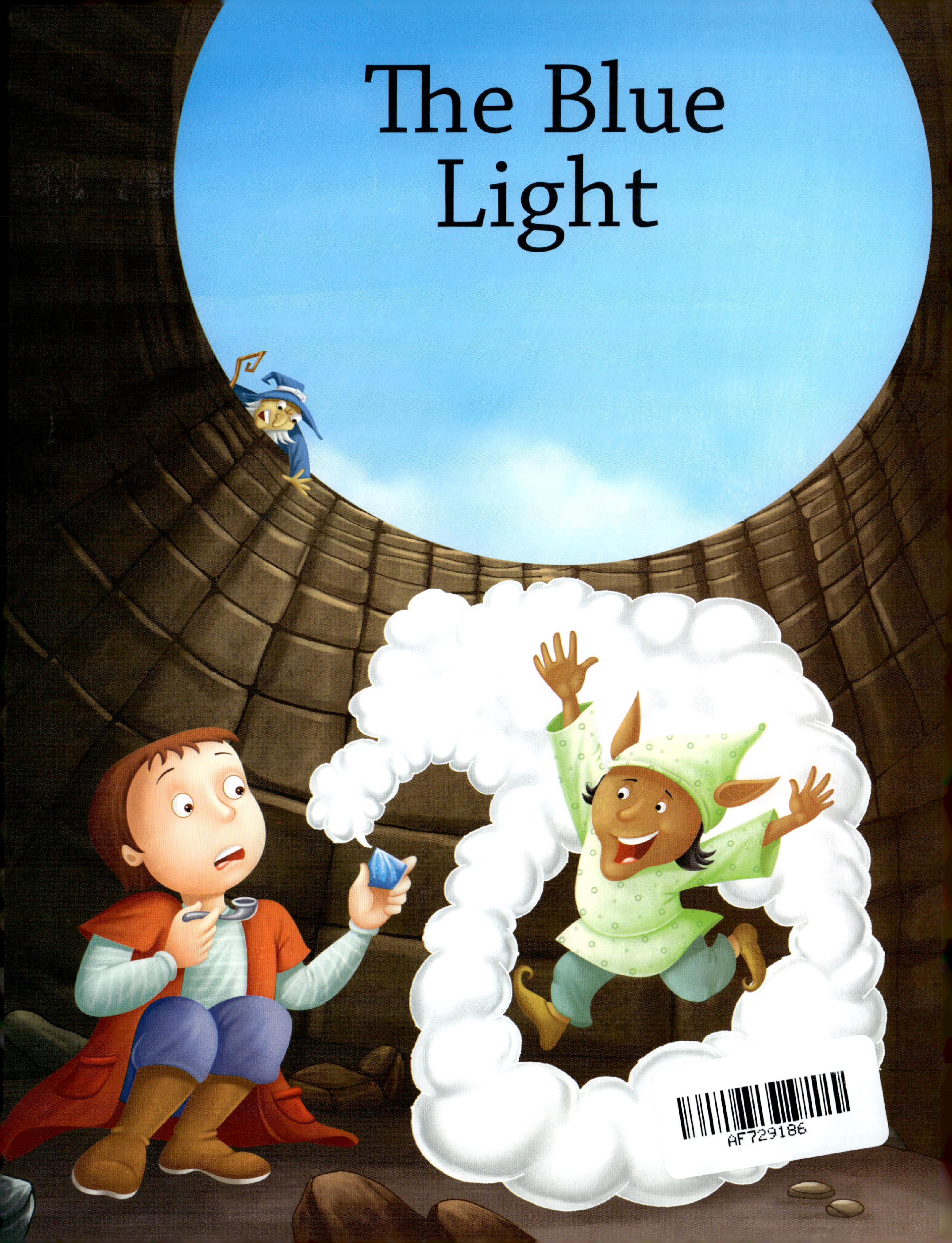

Long ago, there lived a soldier who had faithfully served the king for many years. During a war, he got badly injured and could no longer fight. So, the king dismissed him saying, 'An injured soldier cannot serve my land.' The soldier, who knew nothing but to be a soldier, became sad. On his way homeward he reached a forest.

Deep in the forest the soldier saw a light. He went towards it and soon reached a small house. He knocked on the door. An old witch opened the door. 'Please let me stay here tonight,' pleaded the soldier. 'You can stay, eat and drink here but in return you must dig around my garden, tomorrow,' said the witch. The soldier agreed.

The next day, the soldier dug around the garden all day. He got tired. So, the witch said, 'You can stay here for one more night. In return, you must chop a load of wood into smaller pieces tomorrow.' The soldier agreed. The next day, he chopped the wood till evening and again the witch told him to stay.

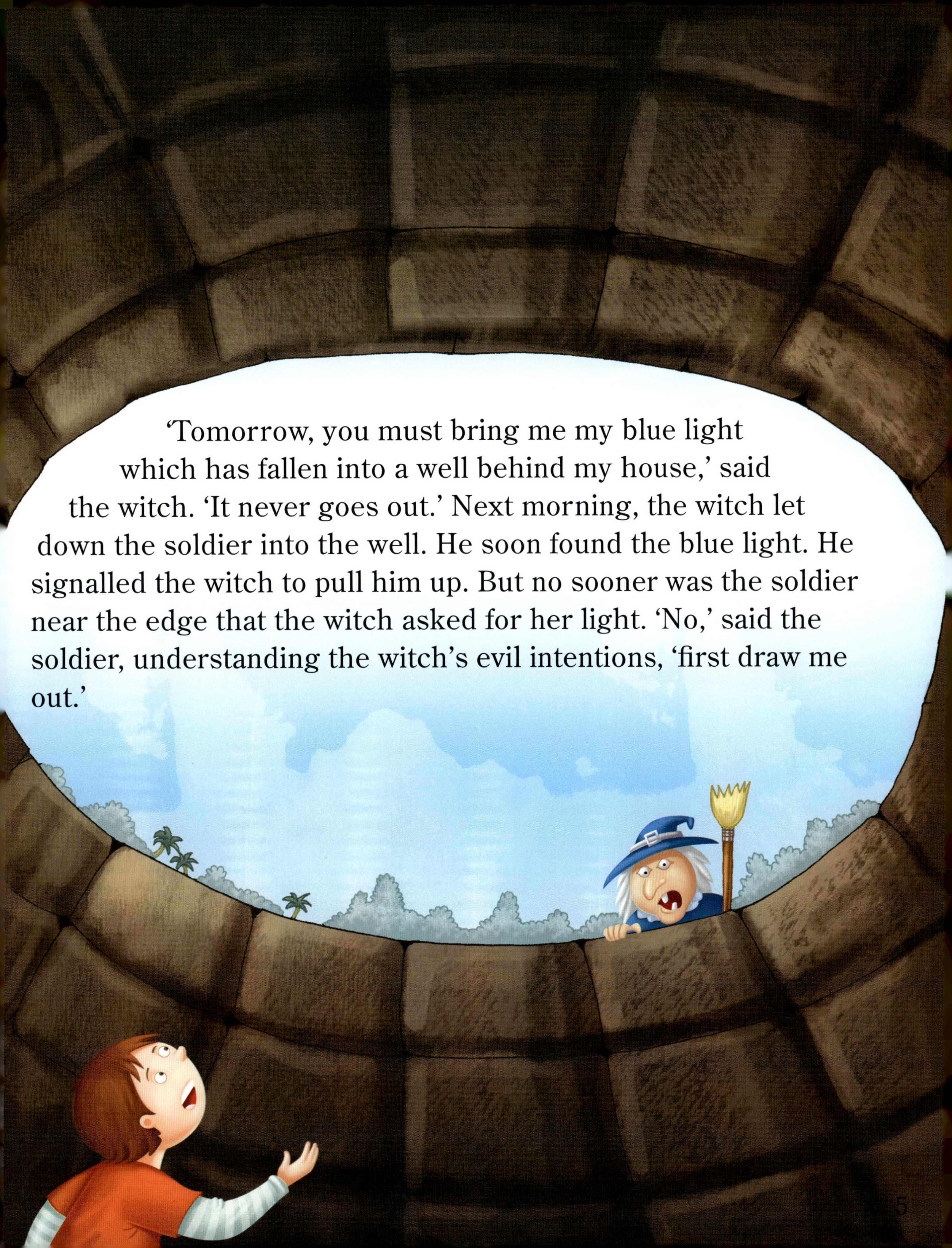

'Tomorrow, you must bring me my blue light which has fallen into a well behind my house,' said the witch. 'It never goes out.' Next morning, the witch let down the soldier into the well. He soon found the blue light. He signalled the witch to pull him up. But no sooner was the soldier near the edge that the witch asked for her light. 'No,' said the soldier, understanding the witch's evil intentions, 'first draw me out.'

Angry, the witch left the soldier inside the well. Thinking that he would soon die, the soldier took out his tobacco pipe. He lit it from the blue light and began to smoke. As the smoke thickened, suddenly a black dwarf stood before him. 'Lord, what are your commands?' 'Take me out of here,' said the soldier.

At once, the dwarf led the soldier out through an underground passage. The soldier took along with him the blue light. On the way, the dwarf showed him the witch's treasures. The soldier took as much as he could carry. Once outside, the soldier told the dwarf, 'Bind the old witch, and carry her before the judge.' In a while, the dwarf returned and said, 'It is all done. What are your next commands?'

'There are no more commands for you at present,' said the soldier.

'Remember to light something at the blue light and I shall come at once,' said the dwarf and vanished.

Happily, the soldier returned to the town, bought beautiful clothes, ate a delicious meal and then lodged in the best inn.

When he was well rested, the soldier lit his pipe at the blue light. At once, the dwarf came. 'I had served the king faithfully, but he dismissed me,' said the soldier. 'What must I do?' asked the dwarf. 'At midnight, when the king's daughter is in bed, bring her here. She shall do the servants' work for me.' 'It is easy thing for me to do,' said the dwarf, 'but a dangerous thing for you if you are discovered.'

As the clock struck midnight, the dwarf brought the princess to the soldier's room. 'Get to your work at once,' said the soldier, seeing the princess. 'Fetch the broom and sweep the chamber.' All through the night, the princess did all the chores with half closed eyes. Just before day break, the dwarf carried the princess back to her bedchamber.

Next morning when the princess woke up, she went up to the king. She said, 'Father, I had a strange dream last night. I was carried through the streets with blinding speed and taken to a soldier's room. There I was made to work like a servant. It was only a dream but I feel so tired as if I have really done everything.'

'It may have happened,' said the king, thoughtfully. 'Princess, fill your pocket with peas and make a small hole in your pocket. If you are carried away again, the peas will fall out leaving behind a trail.' The princess consented. Meanwhile, the dwarf, hidden, had heard everything. At night, when he carried away the sleeping princess, some peas did fall out of her pocket. But they left no trail as the dwarf had craftily scattered peas in every street.

Next morning, when the king sent soldiers to look for the pea trail, their efforts went in vain. Everywhere they looked, the streets were filled with peas. Disappointed, the king asked the princess to leave behind one of her shoes where she was taken. Again the dwarf heard the plot and told the soldier about it. But the soldier said fearlessly, 'Bring the princess.' Later, the princess did as she was instructed.

Next morning, the king had the entire town searched for his daughter's shoe. It was found in the soldier's room and he was thrown into prison. Meanwhile, the soldier had left the blue light in his room. He only had one gold coin in his pocket. Sitting in his prison cell, the soldier had an idea. He stood by the window in his prison and waited. Soon, one of his comrades passed by.

The soldier called his comrade and said, 'Would you be so kind as to fetch my bundle lying in the inn in return for a gold coin.' His comrade soon returned with the bundle and took the gold coin. As soon as the soldier was alone, he lit his pipe and the dwarf came. 'Do not fear,' said the dwarf. 'Go wherever they take you but keep the blue light with you.'

Next day, the soldier was tried and the judge condemned him to death. But before he was killed, the soldier begged a last favour. 'Your Majesty, let me smoke my pipe one last time,' he said. The king agreed. Then, the soldier pulled out his pipe and lighted it at the blue light. At once, the dwarf appeared carrying a cudgel.

‘Strike down the judge and the king who have treated me so unjustly,’ said the soldier. At once, the dwarf fell upon the judge with the cudgel. The king trembled seeing the judge and begged the soldier for mercy. The king was pardoned. He also married his daughter to the soldier and gave him his kingdom. The soldier was never troubled again.